FOR DAD

First edition 2017

Library of Congress Catalog Card Number pending
ISBN 978–0–7636–8146–3

17 18 19 20 21 22 CCP 10 9 8 7 6 5 4 3 2 1

Printed in Shenzhen, Guangdong, China

MIX
Paper from responsible sources
FSC
www.fsc.org FSC® C008047

This book was typeset in Egyptian Extended, Just Another Hand, and Kids Crayon.
The illustrations were done in acrylic paint and pencil on watercolor paper.

Candlewick Press
99 Dover Street
Somerville, Massachusetts 02144

visit us at www.candlewick.com

THINGS TO DO WITH Dad

Sam Zuppardi

CANDLEWICK PRESS

VACUUM THE CARPETS

HANG OUT THE LAUNDRY
Join the circus

More
Things to Do
With Dad
Drive race cars
Explore the ocean
Climb a mountain
visit the moon
Ride a dinosaur
Fly jet packs